GREEN BAY PACKERS

BY DAN MYERS

SportsZone
An Imprint of Abdo Publishing
abdopublishing.com

abdopublishing.com

Published by Abdo Publishing, a division of ABDO, PO Box 398166, Minneapolis, Minnesota 55439.

Printed in the United States of America, North Mankato, Minnesota
042016
092016

Cover Photo: Paul Spinelli/AP Images
Interior Photos: Paul Spinelli/AP Images, 1; James V. Biever/Getty Images, 4-5; Bruce Dierdorff/Getty Images, 6-7; Bettmann/Corbis, 8-9; H. Marc Larson/Green Bay News-Chronicle/AP Images, 10-11; DVN/AP Images, 12-13; Vernon Biever/AP Images, 15, 16-17, 18-19; AP Images, 14; Morry Gash/AP Images, 21, 24-25; Al Messerschmidt/AP Images, 20, 23; Cliff Welch/Icon Sportswire/AP Images, 22; Mike Roemer/AP Images, 26; Tom DiPace/AP Images, 27; Marcio Jose Sanchez/AP Images, 28-29

Editor: Patrick Donnelly
Series Designer: Nikki Farinella

Cataloging-in-Publication Data
Names: Myers, Dan, author.
Title: Green Bay Packers / by Dan Myers.
Description: Minneapolis, MN : Abdo Publishing, [2017] | Series: NFL up close | Includes index.
Identifiers: LCCN 2015960344 | ISBN 9781680782172 (lib. bdg.) | ISBN 9781680776287 (ebook)
Subjects: LCSH: Green Bay Packers (Football team)--History--Juvenile literature. | National Football League--Juvenile literature. | Football--Juvenile literature. | Professional sports--Juvenile literature. | Football teams--Wisconsin--Juvenile literature.
Classification: DDC 796.332--dc23
LC record available at http://lccn.loc.gov/2015960344

TABLE OF CONTENTS

A LEGEND IS BORN

September 20, 1992, was a sunny afternoon in northeast Wisconsin. The Green Bay Packers trailed the Cincinnati Bengals 23-17 with just over a minute left in the game. They had to go 92 yards with no timeouts, and their backup quarterback was in the game.

Impossible? For most, maybe. But on this day, the backup quarterback was Brett Favre. It took five plays and 53 seconds for a legend to be born.

FAST FACT

Brett Favre got his break against the Bengals after starting quarterback Don Majkowski injured his ankle.

Brett Favre prepares to drive the Packers' offense to victory against the Cincinnati Bengals on September 20, 1992.

FAST FACT

In 47 career NFL games, Kitrick Taylor caught just one touchdown pass—the game-winner in Brett Favre's first victory.

Favre led the Packers on an improbable drive. With 13 seconds left, he launched a missile down the right sideline. Wide receiver Kitrick Taylor hauled it in for a 35-yard touchdown. The crowd at Lambeau Field went crazy. Chris Jacke's extra-point kick completed the comeback. Green Bay won 24–23.

The next week, Favre started his first National Football League (NFL) game. He went on to start the next 253 games for Green Bay. Favre threw 442 touchdown passes in 16 seasons with the Packers. He also won a Super Bowl and three NFL Most Valuable Player (MVP) Awards.

Brett Favre gets ready to fire against the Cincinnati Bengals on September 20, 1992.

MORE THAN A STADIUM

Long before Lambeau was the name on the Packers' stadium, Earl "Curly" Lambeau was the team's founder. The Packers began playing in 1919. A local meat packing company gave them money for their uniforms, so Lambeau named the team the Packers. They joined the American Pro Football Association (APFA) in 1921. That league became the NFL in 1922.

From 1921 through 1929, Lambeau was both a player and coach for the Packers. He then coached the team for 20 more seasons. He became one of the NFL's most successful coaches during that time.

FAST FACT

The Packers and the Chicago Bears are the only teams from the NFL's first year still playing in their original cities.

Packers coach Curly Lambeau plots strategy with Tony Canadeo, *3*, Irv Comp, *51*, and Don Hutson, *14*, in 1943.

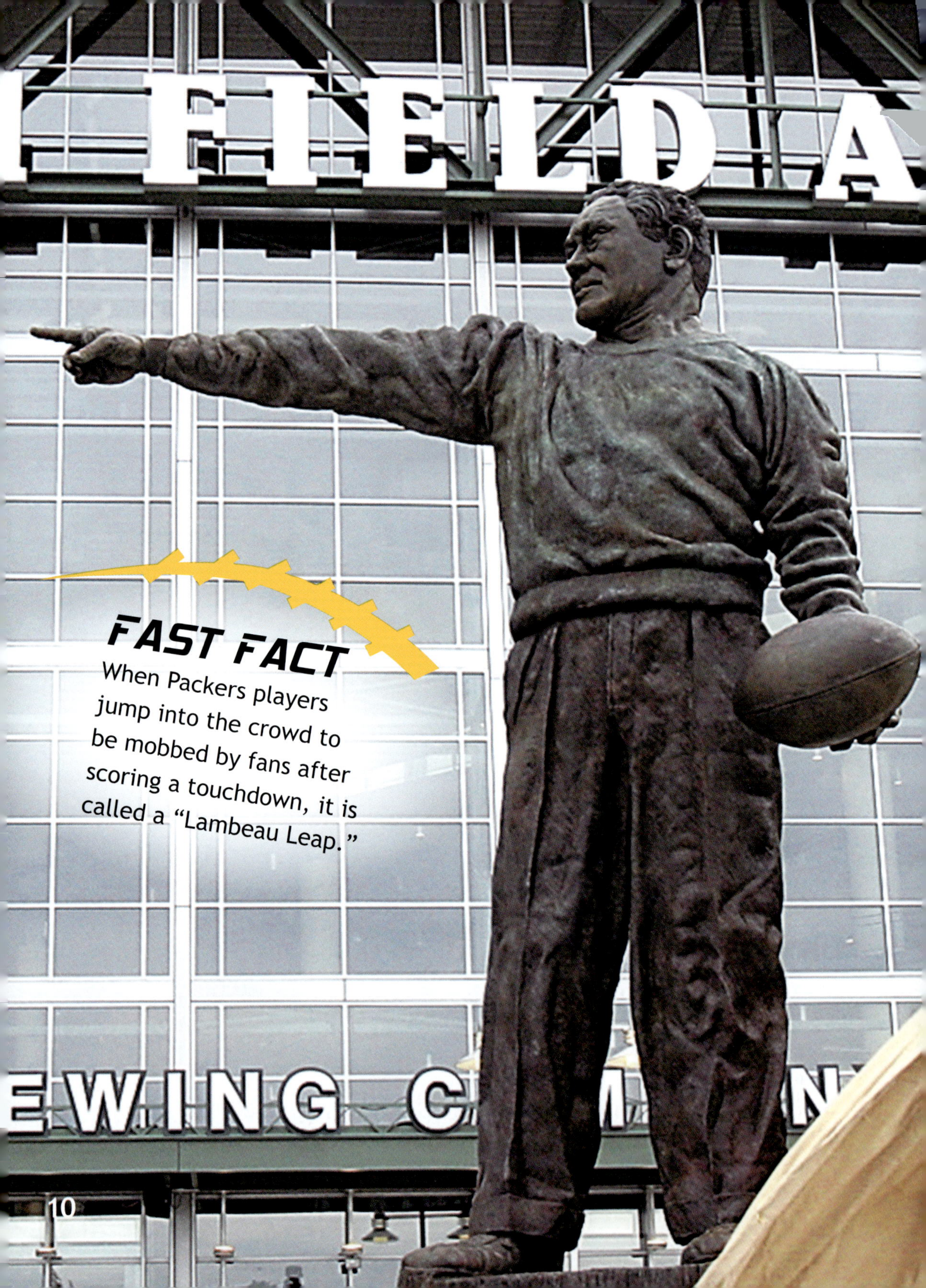

FAST FACT

When Packers players jump into the crowd to be mobbed by fans after scoring a touchdown, it is called a "Lambeau Leap."

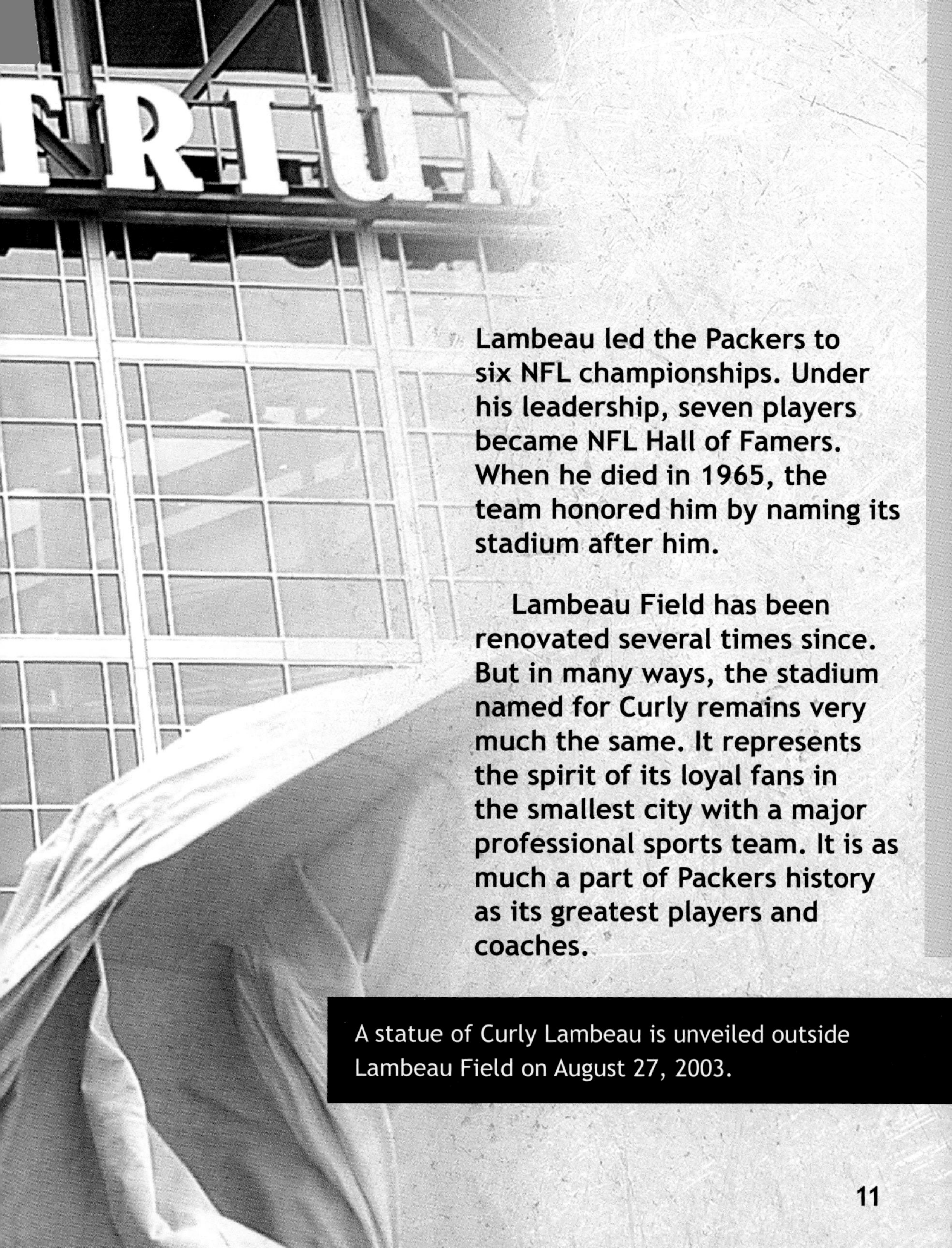

Lambeau led the Packers to six NFL championships. Under his leadership, seven players became NFL Hall of Famers. When he died in 1965, the team honored him by naming its stadium after him.

Lambeau Field has been renovated several times since. But in many ways, the stadium named for Curly remains very much the same. It represents the spirit of its loyal fans in the smallest city with a major professional sports team. It is as much a part of Packers history as its greatest players and coaches.

A statue of Curly Lambeau is unveiled outside Lambeau Field on August 27, 2003.

TITLETOWN

The Packers hired Vince Lombardi as coach in 1959. At the time, many fans must have wondered, "Who is Vince Lombardi?" For many years, Lombardi was a top assistant coach for the New York Giants. But few knew what greatness was in store.

The year before Lombardi came to Green Bay, the Packers finished 1-10-1. It was the worst record in team history. Players and fans were angry. They wanted change. With Lombardi, the Packers' fortunes changed quickly.

FAST FACT

Lombardi coached alongside Tom Landry in New York. Landry went on to lead the Dallas Cowboys to five Super Bowls.

Packers players carry Vince Lombardi off the field after the team clinched the NFL Western Conference title in 1961.

The Packers improved to 7-5 in 1959. Lombardi won NFL Coach of the Year Award for his efforts. The next year, the Packers reached the NFL Championship Game. They lost to the Philadelphia Eagles, but it was a sign of good things to come.

Green Bay won the NFL championship in 1961, 1962, and 1965. Quarterback Bart Starr led the offense. Running backs Jim Taylor and Paul Hornung chewed up yardage behind a powerful offensive line. Fierce linebacker Ray Nitschke led a hard-hitting defense.

Packers linebacker Ray Nitschke, *66*, upends Oakland Raiders running back Hewritt Dixon in Super Bowl II.

Bart Starr waits to be introduced before the 1962 NFL Championship Game at New York's Yankee Stadium.

FAST FACT

People began calling Green Bay "Titletown" because of the many NFL titles the Packers won in the 1960s.

In 1966, the NFL began playing a championship game with the winners of the rival American Football League (AFL). The game was called the Super Bowl.

Lombardi's Packers easily took care of the AFL champion Kansas City Chiefs in January 1967. A year later, the Packers did the same to the Oakland Raiders. That gave the Packers three straight NFL championships. And it was their fifth title in seven years. Few teams in any sport have ever had a run of success to match it.

FAST FACT

Vince Lombardi stopped coaching the Packers after the second Super Bowl. After he died in 1970, the Super Bowl trophy was named in his honor.

Running back Jim Taylor, *31*, attacks the Kansas City Chiefs in Super Bowl I.

FAST FACT

Vince Lombardi's teams went 89-29-4 in the regular season and 9-1 in the playoffs.

LOMBARDI COMES HOME

The Packers quickly went from being the best team in the NFL to one of the worst. Vince Lombardi was gone and the veterans of the 1960s teams retired. From 1968 through 1992, the Packers made the playoffs just twice. Former Packers Bart Starr and Forrest Gregg had unsuccessful stints coaching the team. It seemed nobody could recreate the glory of the Lombardi era.

The rest of the NFL roughed up the Packers throughout the 1970s and 1980s.

Then, the team hired Mike Holmgren as coach. He had coached the high-flying San Francisco 49ers offense for the previous three seasons. Then the Packers traded a first-round draft pick to the Atlanta Falcons for quarterback Brett Favre.

Finally, in 1993 the Packers shocked the football world by signing free agent defensive end Reggie White. The future Hall of Famer was respected around the NFL. He convinced other players that Green Bay was going in the right direction.

Reggie White has San Francisco 49ers quarterback Steve Young on the run in a playoff game on January 6, 1996.

Mike Holmgren was a big part of the Packers' turnaround that began when he arrived in 1992.

FAST FACT

Reggie White won the NFL Defensive Player of the Year award twice—in 1987, when he led the NFL with 21 sacks, and again in 1998, when he was 37 years old.

Favre's magic started making things happen in Green Bay. In 1993, the Packers returned to the playoffs for the first time since 1982. Two years later, they won their division for the first time since 1972.

In 1996, the Packers went 13-3. They cruised through the playoffs. Then they defeated the New England Patriots 35-21 in the Super Bowl. For the first time in almost 30 years, the Vince Lombardi Trophy was back in Green Bay.

Super Bowl MVP Desmond Howard sprints to the end zone on a second-half kickoff return against the New England Patriots.

At long last, the Lombardi Trophy was headed back to Green Bay after the Packers beat the Patriots in the Super Bowl.

FAST FACT

Brett Favre led the NFL in touchdown passes in 1995, 1996, and 1997. He won the Associated Press NFL MVP Award in each of those seasons.

PASSING THE TORCH

The Packers reached the Super Bowl again after the 1997 season, but they lost to the Denver Broncos. They had mixed results for the next decade. Mike Holmgren left Green Bay for Seattle after the 1998 season. He was replaced by Ray Rhodes, who only lasted one year. His replacement, Mike Sherman, took the Packers to the playoffs four times. But they could not advance past the second round.

After a 4-12 season in 2005, the Packers replaced Sherman with another former 49ers coach, Mike McCarthy.

FAST FACT

Before Mike Sherman took over, the Packers had never lost a home playoff game. Under Sherman, they lost playoff games at Lambeau Field twice in three years.

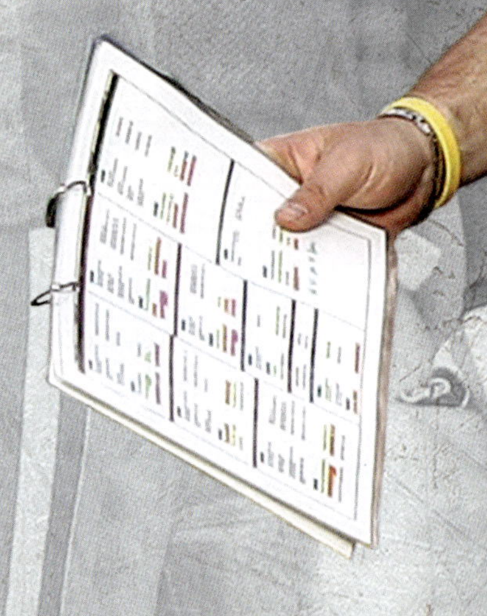

Mike McCarthy was brought in to coach the Packers in 2006.

It was a time of change in Green Bay. Favre was nearing the end of his career. He played his final season in a Packers uniform in 2007, leading the team to within one win of the Super Bowl.

The following season, the Packers became Aaron Rodgers's team. The Packers drafted him in 2005. Then, they let him watch and learn for his first three seasons. It was a rocky transition replacing Favre, a fan favorite and Packers legend. But in Rodgers's third season as Green Bay's starting quarterback, he led the Packers back to the top.

Brett Favre led the Packers on one last playoff run before leaving the team after the 2007 season.

Aaron Rodgers gets ready to air one out against the Pittsburgh Steelers in the Super Bowl.

FAST FACT

Aaron Rodgers was the Super Bowl MVP as the Packers beat the Pittsburgh Steelers 31–25 in February 2011. The win gave Green Bay its fourth Super Bowl victory.

Aaron Rodgers and Mike McCarthy are the latest in a long line of successful quarterback-coach tandems in Green Bay.

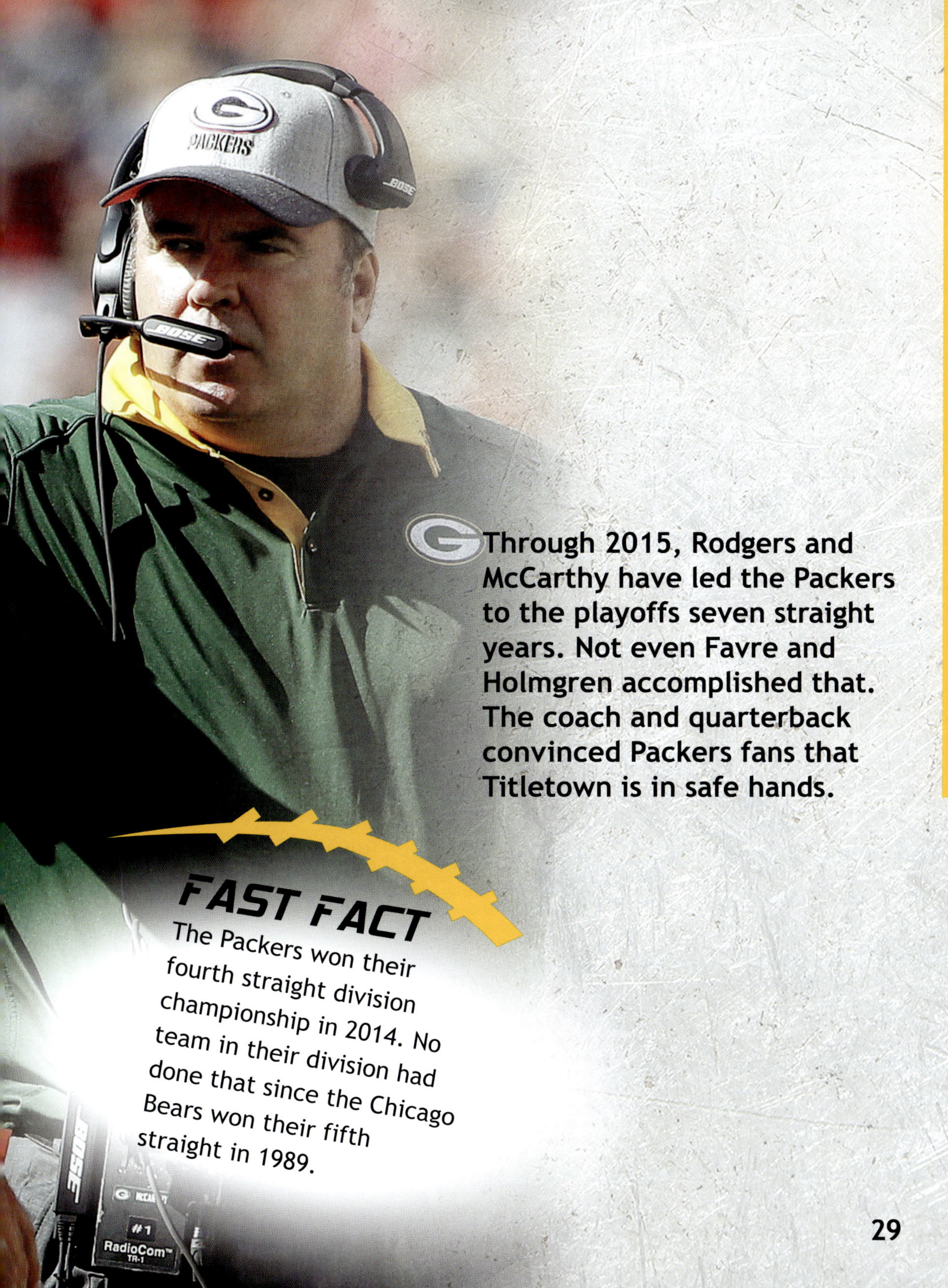

Through 2015, Rodgers and McCarthy have led the Packers to the playoffs seven straight years. Not even Favre and Holmgren accomplished that. The coach and quarterback convinced Packers fans that Titletown is in safe hands.

FAST FACT

The Packers won their fourth straight division championship in 2014. No team in their division had done that since the Chicago Bears won their fifth straight in 1989.

TIMELINE

1921
The Packers join the APFA, which became the National Football League.

1929
The Packers win their first of 13 NFL championships and the first of six under Curly Lambeau.

1961
The Packers win their seventh world championship in Vince Lombardi's third season as coach.

1967
On January 15, Green Bay defeats the Kansas City Chiefs 35-10 in the first Super Bowl.

1968
The Packers defeat the Oakland Raiders 33-14 on January 14 to win the second Super Bowl. Lombardi retires from coaching the team later that year.

1992
Coach Mike Holmgren and quarterback Brett Favre arrive in Green Bay.

1993
The Packers return to the playoffs for the first time in more than a decade.

1997
On January 26, Green Bay beats the New England Patriots in the Super Bowl.

2005
In the first round of the NFL Draft, the Packers select quarterback Aaron Rodgers to be Favre's eventual replacement.

2011
On February 6, Rodgers leads the Packers past the Pittsburgh Steelers in the Super Bowl.

GLOSSARY

COMEBACK
When a team losing a game rallies to win.

DIVISION
A group of teams that help form a league.

EXTRA POINT
A kick attempted after a touchdown. It is worth one point.

FREE AGENT
A player who is free to sign with any team.

PLAYOFFS
A set of games after the regular season that decides which team will be the champion.

RETIRE
To withdraw from a job or occupation.

SACK
A tackle of the quarterback behind the line of scrimmage before he can pass the ball.

VETERAN
A player who has played many years.

INDEX

ABOUT THE AUTHOR

Dan Myers was raised in Eagan, Minnesota, and graduated with a degree in journalism from Minnesota State University. He has covered sports at all levels in the Twin Cities since 2008. He and his wife live in Hudson, Wisconsin, with their beagle, Kato.